Ollie Bear's

Adventures with the Rainbow Heart Light

Connections

Written by Tracey O'Mara

Illustrated by Sherae Kim

Balboa Press books may be ordered through booksellers or by contacting:

Balboa Press
A Division of Hay House
1663 Liberty Drive
Bloomington, IN 47403
www.balboapress.com
1 (877) 407-4847

ISBN: 978-1-5043-2559-2 (sc)
ISBN: 978-1-5043-2558-5 (e)

Library of Congress Control Number: 2014922499

Printed in the United States of America.

Balboa Press rev. date: 12/17/2014

BALBOA.
PRESS
A DIVISION OF HAY HOUSE

Once upon a time in a quaint little town called Joyville, a beautiful baby bear was born. His name was Ollie Bear.

Now, Ollie Bear was born with a broken heart. Mommy Bear and Daddy Bear were very sad because they did not know how to fix it. So, Mommy Bear and Daddy Bear went to see Grandma Bear for comfort.

Mommy Bear and Daddy Bear told Grandma Bear all about Ollie Bear's broken heart. Grandma Bear knew exactly what to say. She told them the story of the Rainbow Heart Light.

"The Rainbow Heart Light," Grandma Bear said, "is a beautiful blessing from the Angel Bears sent to look after all the little bears. We can use the colors of the Rainbow Heart Light to help everyone.

We are going to use the Rainbow Heart Light to wrap
Ollie Bear up in a beautiful bright pink color.

The pink color is to let him know that he is loved and to help keep him safe throughout the challenges in his life."

Mommy Bear and Daddy Bear still did not understand. They asked Grandma Bear, "but how can a color help someone?"

Grandma Bear, who was a very wise bear, said, "The Rainbow Heart Light has guardian angels, two of them are called Clair Bear and Sarah Bear. They will take all the little blessings of the colors and send them to the little bear that needs help."

The next day, Mommy Bear and Daddy Bear took Ollie Bear to the hospital so that Dr. Starr Bear could mend his broken heart.

They remembered what Grandma Bear said about the
Rainbow Heart Light. They closed their eyes and thought
of a bright pink light filled with all the love in their hearts.
The angels Clair Bear and Sarah Bear took the light and gave
some of it to Dr. Starr Bear to help mend Ollie Bear's heart
and some of it to Ollie Bear to help him heal quickly.

Now with a perfect heart, Ollie Bear is ready for his own adventures with the Rainbow Heart Light.

Grandma Bear's Guide

How to Use the Colors of the Rainbow Heart Light

Grandma Bear likes to use certain colors for different things, but you can use any color that you like.

Step 1: "First, pick a color"

Step 2: "close your eyes"

Step 3: "imagine that color is filled with all of the love in your heart"

Step 4: "think of the person, this can be even yourself, animal, or situation you would like to help"

Step 5: "picture that person, animal, or situation surrounded by that color"

Grandma Bear's Color Chart:

Pink for any little bear (person) that isn't feeling very well, is worried, or going through a difficult time in their life.

Purple to inspire ourselves and others to use our creative gifts.

Blue to help ourselves and others feel calm in uncomfortable situations and to help all of the creatures in the ocean.

Green is very soothing and healing. You can use Green for someone that is injured and all the animals and plants on the earth.

Yellow to spread happiness. It helps us to feel happy and goofy. You can also send yellow to help all of the little bumble bees, after all, they have a very important job to do!

Orange is for joy and laughter. It also gives us all energy and helps to empower and uplift our spirits.

Red is to help us and others feel strong in any situation and helps us feel protected in challenging times.

Gold and White to send to all of our loved ones that are no longer here on earth with us.

Turquoise is a special color we can send to ourselves. Using turquoise, we can wrap ourselves up with love and it reminds us that we are all perfect just the way we are.

CPSIA information can be obtained at www.ICGtesting.com
Printed in the USA
LVOW05s0816110215

426575LV00008B/23/P